Wee Granny's Magic Bag
and the
Pirates

Elizabeth McKay
& Maria Bogade

To Robbie, Rachel and Erin, with love – E.M.

To Leon, to many big and magical adventures – M.B.

Kelpies is an imprint of Floris Books. First published in 2018 by Floris Books. Text © 2018 Elizabeth McKay
Illustrations © 2018 Maria Bogade. Elizabeth McKay and Maria Bogade assert their right under the
Copyright, Designs and Patents Act 1988 to be recognised as the Author and Illustrator of this Work. All rights reserved
No part of this book may be reproduced without prior permission of Floris Books, Edinburgh www.florisbooks.co.uk
The publisher acknowledges subsidy from Creative Scotland towards the publication of this volume
British Library CIP Data available. ISBN 978-178250-475-7 Printed in Poland

This book
belongs to

_____

_____

_____

Harry and Emily were going to Arran for their holidays with Wee Granny. They were excited to see she'd brought her tartan bag.
"Wee Granny," said Emily, "have you got anything special in your bag today?"
"Well," she replied, "I've got my binoculars and our picnic lunch."

The children were disappointed. Usually Wee Granny had much more interesting things inside her bag.

Once when they went camping, Emily forgot her sleeping bag. Wee Granny opened her tartan bag and brought out...

... a comfy bed with fluffy pillows.

Wee Granny and the children set off on their holiday,
but when they reached the terminal, they saw their ferry
sailing out to sea.

"Oh no, we've missed the boat!" cried Emily.

"We'll have to wait a whole day for the next one," said Harry.

"Och, don't worry, my bonnie darlings," said Wee Granny,
reaching into her tartan bag and bringing out...

"... a rowing boat!" said Harry.

"I thought this might come in handy."
Wee Granny pulled four lifejackets from
her bag as well. "All aboard!"

They'd just lost sight of the mainland
when Emily said, "My feet feel all soggy!"
"We've sprung a leak!" yelled Harry.

"Keep calm, my bonnie darlings," said Wee Granny.
"We'll head for that island over there."
"We'll sink before we reach it!" panicked Harry.
Wee Granny searched inside her tartan bag. "Not if we use..."

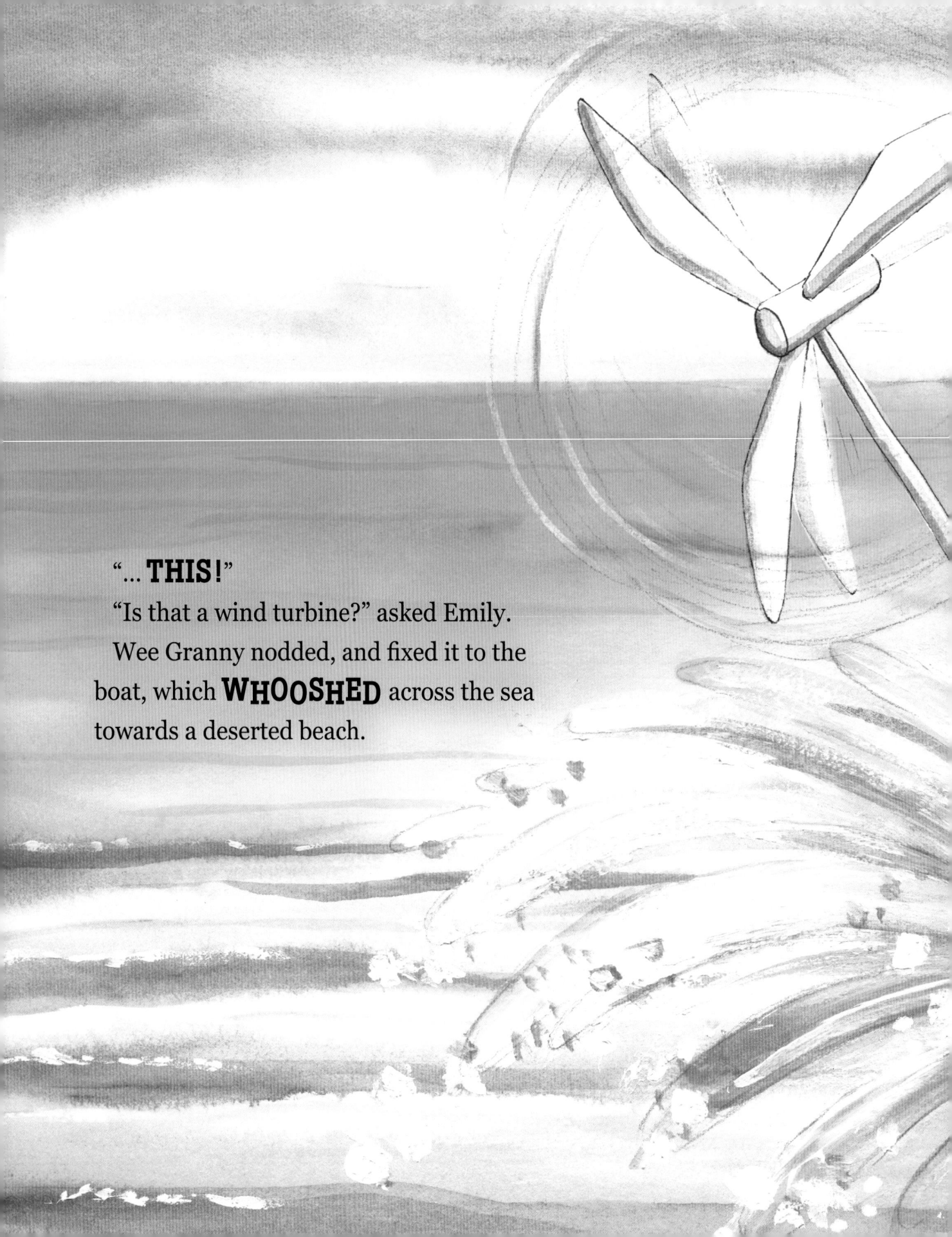

"... **THIS!**"

"Is that a wind turbine?" asked Emily.

Wee Granny nodded, and fixed it to the boat, which **WHOOSHED** across the sea towards a deserted beach.

"It's going too fast!" shrieked Emily.
"We're going to..."

CRASH!

"We've been shipwrecked," Harry sighed as they scrambled out of the boat.

"Don't worry," said Wee Granny, "I've got just the thing to cheer us up." She rummaged in her tartan bag and brought out...

"Sandwiches?" Harry was disappointed.

"We can't make plans on empty stomachs."
Wee Granny laid out their picnic.

While they were eating their lunch, Harry
borrowed Wee Granny's binoculars to look for seals.

"Can you see any?" asked Emily.

"No, but I can see something else... something
coming this way. It looks like..."

"... PIRATES! And they're coming ashore!"

"Ahoy there, landlubbers!" called their captain.
"Arrr be Cap'n Shoogle of the *Clootie Dumplin*."
"An arrr be Jack," said a boy pirate.
"We're searchin' for buried treasure."

"We can help you look," said Emily, "if you give us a lift to Arran."

"Arrr that sounds a fair bargain," agreed Captain Shoogle. "Jack, fetch the map."

"Sorry, Cap'n," said Jack, "arrrs left it at home."

"**ARRRRRRRR!**" roared the captain.

"Now don't get crabbit." Wee Granny peered inside her tartan bag. "Try this instead..."

"FESTERIN' FROGS!"
said Captain Shoogle. "A metal
detector! We'll find the booty in
a shake of a cat's flea."

Everyone followed Captain Shoogle
as he stomped across the sand with the
metal detector.

They scrambled over rocks...

beep beep beep

disappeared inside caves...

beep beep beep

then came out again...

BEEP BEEP BEEP BEEP BEEP

"Jack, fetch the spades!" yelled the captain.

"Sorry, Cap'n," said Jack, "arrrs left them at home."

"Arrrrrrrr!" growled Captain Shoogle.

"Don't worry," said Wee Granny, hunting inside her bag until she found...

"Wow!" said Harry and Emily.

"Crumblin' cockroaches!" said Captain Shoogle.

"Jumpin' jellyfish!" said Jack.

"**SHIVER ME TIMBERS!**" chorused the other pirates.

Wee Granny climbed into the driver's seat of the digger and switched on the engine.

It didn't take long to dig up the treasure chest
buried in the sand.

"Diamonds," said Captain Shoogle.

"Rubies," said Emily, "and sapphires, and emeralds, and..."

"… **GOLD!**" Harry could hardly believe his eyes.

"Thanks for yer help, me hearties," said Captain Shoogle.
"Now would yerrrs like to join arrr crew?"

"That's very kind of you," said Wee Granny, "but we're
late for our holidays in Arran."

"You said you'd take us," Harry reminded him.

"So arrr did, and Cap'n Shoogle always keeps his word. Ready the *Clootie Dumplin*!" he ordered the crew. "Set sail for Arrrran!"

Harry and Emily both had a shot at steering while Wee Granny snoozed in a hammock.

Jack kept lookout from high up in the crow's nest. After a while they heard him shout out,

"LAND AHOY!"

"Anchors away!" yelled Captain Shoogle.
"We've reached Arrrran!"

The pirates helped Harry and Emily
climb down from the ship.

'I'm not very keen on wobbly ladders," said Wee Granny. "I'll just see where this goes..."

"You're walkin' the plank!" yelled Jack.
"Stop! You'll fall into the sea!" warned Harry.
"Don't worry, my bonnie darlings."
Wee Granny reached into her tartan bag and pulled out...

... a trampoline!

"Leapin' lizards!" gasped Captain Shoogle
as Wee Granny walked the plank, bounced
on the trampoline, did a triple somersault
and landed on the pier.

As the new friends said goodbye, they heard a loud rumble.

"Canons!" yelled Captain Shoogle. "Take cover, me hearties, werrr under attack!"

"Don't worry, Cap'n," Jack laughed, "it's just my stomach rumblin'. Arrrs hungry."

"**SO ARRR WE!!!**" roared all the other pirates.

"Poor souls," tutted Wee Granny. "Let's have some tea before we go."

She opened her bag and tugged and tugged until out came...

... a fish and chip van.

"**SHIVER ME TIMBERS!**" yelled the pirates.

Soon everyone was sitting on the harbour wall singing sea shanties and eating their fish suppers. All except Jack, who looked fair scunnered.

"Arrrs a rubbish pirate," he sighed. "Arrrs always forgettin' things."

"Maybe I can help," said Wee Granny. She opened her bag...

... and out flew a parrot.

"His name's Macblether," said Wee Granny. "He's good at remembering things."

"Thanks," said Jack, "arrrs a proper pirate at last. Can I ask yer somethin', Wee Granny? Is yer bag magic?"

"Is yer bag magic?" echoed Macblether.

"Is it?" asked Harry.

"Please tell us," begged Emily.

"I can't tell you, me hearties," Wee Granny replied. "Not for all the gold aboard the *Clootie Dumplin*."